"Why do you think there's a ghost in Mr. Horvath's house?" I asked. Mr. Horvath's house is large and run-down with all kinds of bends and corners that jut out, like a person with too many elbows and knees. It was painted a dark green color that looked black in the fading light of the setting sun.

"Vibrations," Spitt replied. "It produces ghostly vibrations that my inner spirit is sensitive to."

I studied the dark hulking house, the black windows, and the silent yard. Maybe Spitt was right. There *was* something behind that window.

# THE TROUBLE WITH SPITT

# VICKI BLUM

Published by
Deseret Book Company
Salt Lake City, Utah

*To my children: Malan, Ginger, Dallin, and Radelle*
*And to Gabe, whose life story I borrowed from*

**Library of Congress Cataloging-in-Publication Data**

Blum, Vicki, 1955–
   The trouble with Spitt / by Vicki Blum.
      p.   cm.
   Summary: Sixth-graders and best friends Kevin and Spitt get to know an elderly man who lives nearby and even become the conduit through which he joins the Mormon Church.
   ISBN 1-57345-147-9 (pb)
   [1. Friendship—Fiction. 2. Old age—Fiction. 3. Mormons—Fiction.] I. Title.
PZ7.B6258Tr    1996
[Fic]—dc20
                                     96-73
                                     CIP
                                     AC

Printed in the United States of America

10  9  8  7  6  5  4  3  2  1

# ❦ CHAPTER 1 ❦

"There's a ghost in the house next door," said Spitt.

I was sitting under the cottonwood tree in Spitt's backyard. It had started to shed fluff, and every so often a piece would float past my nose and make me sneeze. I stretched out on my back and squinted up at Spitt as he hung head-down by his legs, which were hooked over a branch.

"Your eyes are turning red," I said.

"You're not listening."

"How did you guess?"

Spitt Wilburson is my very best friend, and we get along great most of the time, but every now and then he gets a bit carried away. For example, lately one of his favorite things has been to search for evidence of life after death. This was all brought on by his dog, who recently went chasing after a car and got hit by one of the back tires. I

1

feel sorry for the dog, but my sympathy for Spitt has been rapidly disappearing in direct proportion to the amount of time he spends talking about it.

Spitt grabbed the branch with both hands and plopped to the ground. He stood and glared at me while his hair settled to his head, a result of the sudden change in his position in relation to the gravitational pull of the earth.

"You're being too scientific, Kevin," he said. He always says that to me. I think it bothers him that I get good grades in every subject, especially in math, and his only decent marks are in English, and that's only because he's so good at telling stories that aren't true.

"I am not," I said. "I just don't happen to believe in ghosts."

"What if I can prove it?"

"You can't."

"I can prove there's a ghost in Mr. Horvath's house."

I rolled over and sat up. "All right," I said, "I'm listening."

Spitt grinned. He figured he had me completely hooked into believing there really was a ghost, but he was wrong. I was only mildly

2

interested, from a scientific point of view. Big Rock School has a science fair every year, and Spitt's ghost might be an interesting thesis for a project. No one I knew had ever done a project on the scientific evidence of ghosts in High River.

"We'll stake out the house," Spitt said, "and set up shifts. You take the first. I'll take the second. We'll have to check the place out first so we know our way around. It's very important not to get lost when you're doing this type of investigation. We'll go tonight."

Spitt always assumes everyone is as free as he is. His parents both work, so he can do a lot of things I could never get away with. Sometimes he goes out after dark, but I can never get past my mom, who has ears that are able to pick up the sound of sneakers touching carpet at thirty yards through a brick wall.

"Sure," I said, "as long as we're back early." I have another reason for insisting on that. I would never admit it to Spitt, but I don't like the dark. Sometimes when I'm walking home late at night and I'm alone, I start to sweat and shake. I always leave my bedroom curtains open because the street light just outside shines into my room. I could never tell this to Spitt, or the next thing I'd know all the students at Big Rock School would be laughing and making rude remarks.

We talked some more and got things all arranged, and then I went home for supper. An hour later I was back.

"Why do you think there's a ghost in Mr. Horvath's house?" I asked. We were crouched behind the white picket fence that separates Spitt's yard from the one next door. Mr. Horvath's house is large and run-down with all kinds of bends and corners that jut out, like a person with too many elbows and knees. It was painted a dark green color that looked black in the fading light of the setting sun.

"Vibrations," he said. "It produces ghostly vibrations that my inner spirit is sensitive to."

"Your inner spirit is worse off than I thought," I said.

"Look, there's no one home."

I studied the dark hulking house, the black windows, the silent yard. Even the tree was still, as if waiting.

I hesitated. "I saw something behind that window."

"What window?"

"That one." I pointed.

"You're just chickening out at the last minute."

"I am not."

Spitt leaped over the fence, and I followed reluctantly, wondering if a science project on the eating habits of yellow and white butterflies might be less difficult. We tiptoed through the garden and across the grass. We reached the tree and stood under it, looking up. It was a crab apple tree, with branches that were too high to reach and too skinny to hold us, even if we did happen to get up.

"We can get a better view from up there," said Spitt. "Let me climb on your shoulders."

We've been through that before. Spitt is taller and heavier than I am, and I can usually hold him for about five seconds. There's no use trying to talk him out of it, though. Maybe he keeps hoping I've gained weight. We went through our usual routine and ended up in a tangle of arms and legs all over the ground.

"Okay," he said, as if a new light had dawned. "You climb on my shoulders, then."

I made it all the way up and caught a branch.

5

I swung off his shoulders, hooked my legs over the branch, and pulled myself up. The tree wobbled like a stick in a storm.

"You see anything?"

"I could if this tree would stop swinging."

"Well, quit jumping around, then."

I tried not to move, but it didn't help. I looked around as best I could. Things were pretty much the same up here as they had been down below. I noticed one of the upstairs windows was open, and a curtain billowed with the breeze. There seemed to be a light on somewhere deep inside the house. "It's too dark to see anything," I said.

All was quiet, except for the rustling of leaves around my head.

"It's too dark to see anything."

All was quiet.

"Spitt?"

I peered down and spied my loyal and brave friend, Spitt Wilburson, already over the fence and sprinting like a champion of the fifty-yard dash. "Come back!" I yelled. "Come back right now!"

A door slammed. I huddled behind a branch and tried to make my body as skinny as it would go. I pulled a clump of leaves down in front of my face and peeked out between them, but my hands shook and the leaves rattled. I could hardly breathe. I hoped Mr. Horvath wouldn't find me. Maybe he would think I was a woodpecker or a chipmunk crouching up in the branches munching on an acorn. I pulled one of the twigs aside. I looked down below me and saw him standing there looking up.

# ≋ CHAPTER 2 ≋

I held my breath, hoping Mr. Horvath wouldn't notice me. I had never met him before, and I knew this wasn't the way to make a good first impression.

Mr. Horvath had just moved in beside Spitt two weeks ago and Spitt, who has seen him twice, says he's very grumpy and tries to avoid people. My mom told me he came to Alberta from Hungary many years ago and has no family. My sister Cindy says he's a criminal and kidnaps boys to sell as slaves in mainland China to work in the rice fields and wait on rich old members of the last imperial dynasty. I didn't bother telling her, but I don't believe people can get away with that anymore. There are too many policemen and secret agents running around. Besides, you can't believe anything that comes from my sister Cindy.

"Come down right now!" he barked.

I dropped to the ground and stood with my back to the tree. Mr. Horvath was thin and short, hardly taller than I am. He seemed to be all bones, like he would creak if he moved, and his clothes just kind of hung on him, like they do in your closet. He was wearing an old straw hat that was squished flat as if he had jumped on it, and he had bushy white eyebrows and a mustache that drooped over his cheeks like the tusks of a walrus—only right at this moment, not a happy walrus. His jaw was tight, and I could see his hands clenched into fists at his sides.

"I'm sorry, sir," I managed to mumble. If I lived through this, I would certainly have a few things to say to Spitt, and they wouldn't all be polite. Sometimes you have to be firm with Spitt or he'll stomp all over you.

"What's your name?"

"Kevin Thompson."

"What were you doing in the tree?"

"My cat was up there."

"Where's your cat now?"

"She got down and ran away."

"I see."

I hate lying. It really is the worst thing I can

think of to do, but how could I tell him I was up in his tree looking for a ghost?

"Next time tell me when your cat is in the tree," he said, glaring at me and rubbing his chin with his hand.

"Yes, sir," I said.

"You can run along now."

"Yes, sir."

I made it home in fifteen seconds flat. I went in the back door so I could avoid my mom, who would be waiting at the front. She was waiting at the back. I should have known. She has always been able to read my mind. She knows whenever I've done something wrong, and she can tell if I'm really sick or if I'm just pretending. She never lets me get away with anything. The nearest I can figure is she's got ESP, or else she's planted a microphone somewhere on my person. What else could I do? I told her the truth.

I stopped Spitt later that evening as he was riding past the front of my house. "My mom says I have to apologize to Mr. Horvath for lying," I said.

Spitt lifted his left eyebrow. "So?"

"Spitt," I said, "you've got to come with me. It's a matter of honor."

"No," he said. He lifted his bike from the ground and swung back up onto the seat.

"Remember the time I saved you by admitting I was the one who put the dead worm in the teacher's desk drawer?"

"No," he said, placing his right foot on the right pedal.

"Remember the time you fell in the frog pond and I pulled you out with a piece of branch?"

"No," he said. The bike was moving off with him on it.

"All right!" I shouted. "If that's the way you want it! But when Mom takes me to Calaway Park tomorrow, I'll invite Stevie Fisbull instead of you!"

"Calaway Park?" The bike tires skidded across the dirt.

"Yes. Calaway Park. Rides and cotton candy and hot dogs with mustard."

"Why didn't you say so in the first place?" he snapped. "Really, Kevin, you should learn to stop babbling and get to the point of what you are trying to say. It would make a lot of difference in your life."

"Yes," I said. "I really should."

I woke up at 6:37 the next morning and couldn't get back to sleep. I had dreamed about Calaway Park. I had dreamed about a purple monster with green eyes who was ten feet tall and looked just like Mr. Horvath. It had escaped from the haunted house and was chasing me and Spitt all around the park, and the bad part was nobody could see it but us.

After I tossed and wiggled for an hour, I got up and put on my clothes. If my mom saw me up and dressed so early she might take back some of the things she says about me. She says I'm the most unmotivated person she's ever seen. She says you can't move me with a bulldozer, except where there's mischief involved, or food. I think she has judged me wrongly. She hasn't given me a fair chance to prove what I'm really capable of. But then, mothers are like that.

"Come for breakfast," said Mom, poking her head through the doorway. "It's almost ready."

Breakfast was toast and fried eggs. I wish she hadn't done that to me. I hate fried eggs. When they're soft they make me gag, and when they're hard they gum up into a ball on the roof

12

of my mouth and won't go down. I drank three glasses of milk with the first bite.

"You will apologize to Mr. Horvath before we leave," said Mom.

My mom has big brown eyes that have X-ray vision and is built short and skinny, but don't let that fool you. She can still beat me in an arm wrestle and catch up with me whenever I'm running to get away. I think she must have been an Olympic track star when she was a teenager and just hasn't bothered to admit it. I usually try to maintain a good relationship with her whenever possible.

"Okay, Mom," I said.

"What were you doing in the tree?" asked Cindy. Cindy is my little sister. She's only nine years old, but already she's blossomed into a first-rate pest. I hate to think about when she turns ten.

"Nothing," I said.

The doorbell rang. Spitt stood behind it in blue jeans and a red shirt and the hard hat I gave him for his last birthday. He had on his cleats, the ones he wears when he's playing baseball and wants to cover the bases in record time.

13

"Are you ready?" he asked.

"What are you dressed like that for?"

"I'm prepared for the action," he said.

"How are you, Spitt?" said Mom. "How is your mother?"

"Fine."

"Is she working today?"

"No," said Spitt. "She went shopping."

Mom always shows an interest in Spitt and his family. She invites them over for dinner and sometimes for family home evening. Spitt's parents are inactive members of the Church, but Spitt has been coming to church with me for a while now. Mom says it's good for us to have each other. I think she's being a little optimistic. Spitt thinks she's the smartest person in the world.

"Let's go to Mr. Horvath's," I said to Spitt.

"We'll be waiting here when you get back," said Mom, smiling. She always smiles like that when I have to right some wrong I've done or when she thinks I've learned some valuable lesson. I was still trying to redeem myself, so I made sure Spitt didn't bang the door behind us as we went out.

# ✦ CHAPTER 3 ✦

"This is a rare opportunity," said Spitt as we headed toward Mr. Horvath's. "I never realized it when you asked me yesterday, but I've thought it over . . . "

"Forget it," I said. "We're not going over to search for a ghost. We'll apologize, and then we'll leave."

"Why don't you apologize while I take a look around?"

The day was too nice to spend it arguing with Spitt. The sky was clear as a mountain stream, like you could drink it, and the sun was warm but not hot. I don't like it when your clothes stick to your skin and your mouth gets all dry and puckered inside. We walked through someone's yard where the cottonwood and weeping willow hung down over our heads. A squirrel chattered. Sunlight flickered down through the leaves. The hue of the grass and shrubs was like a splash of green paint.

"Summer is the best time," I said.

"I like winter too," said Spitt.

"It's a bit cold."

"Not for me."

"What about when it gets to be forty below?"

Spitt looked right at me, his brow wrinkled sternly. "You're just not tough enough, Kevin," he said.

We walked up Mr. Horvath's broken sidewalk. The garden had plants growing in between the rows. The lawn looked like a field of hay. A robin twittered, as if daring us to come closer.

I knocked on the porch door, and it swung open. It wasn't much of a door, just a few boards with some wire screen in the middle and rusty hinges that creaked.

"Nobody's home," said Spitt.

I dug into my pocket. "I'll leave a note, then," I said. "I'm not coming back to this house. It gives me a funny feeling."

"Those are the vibrations I told you about," said Spitt.

In my pocket were the rough draft of my

essay on bloodsuckers and the broken end of a pencil. I spread the unused side of the paper across my leg and scribbled an apology to Mr. Horvath. "Dear sir," I began. "I am sorry I didn't tell the truth. I don't have a cat. I was looking for a ghost for my friend, Spitt Wilburson, but as you know, there is no such thing." I signed it Kevin Thompson. I folded it neatly three times.

"I'm going to stick it in the door to the house," I said to Spitt. "You stay here."

I tiptoed across the porch with Spitt trailing behind me. I stuffed the note between the inside door and the wall. The door squeaked and swung open, leaving the note still in my hand.

The first thing I saw through the open doorway was a stove, the kind you put wood into. I wouldn't have been certain except I saw one just like it in a museum when our social studies class went on a field trip. There were shelves built into the wall. They held all kinds of things: cans of vegetables, jars of fruit, plates and cups, and some photographs. I was too far away to see what the photographs were of. A fridge stood against one wall, and in the middle of the room was a square wooden table with only three legs. The fourth corner was held up by a stack of cinderblock. Mr. Horvath sat at the table with his head in his hands staring down, but there was nothing there.

"Get back," I whispered to Spitt.

Spitt went blundering past me and did just what I was afraid he might do. His right foot hit a stool that lay on the floor in our way and sent it clattering. Then he clutched his toe and hopped and yelped like a whipped dog. I grabbed his face and covered his mouth with my hand, but it was too late. Mr. Horvath jumped up.

Mr. Horvath's hat was gone, and his mustache drooped over his pale cheeks like it was too heavy for his face. A tuft of white hair stood up at the back of his head like a lone feather. He reminded me of a skinny old bird that is almost finished being plucked.

"How do you do?" I said. His look of surprise was rapidly turning to anger, so I knew I didn't have much time to explain. "I wrote you a note, sir . . . Mr. Horvath," I said, as quickly as the words would come out. "I thought you weren't home so I brought it to leave in the door. See?

Here it is." I placed the note right in front of him and backed up. Spitt was in my way again, and I stepped on his sore foot going back. He yelped again.

Mr. Horvath read the note. It didn't take long—he just sort of glanced down. Spitt always says it amazes him how fast some people can read. I tell him if he would read once in a while he would get good at it too.

Mr. Horvath's lips started to quiver. At first I thought he was getting his facial muscles all tensed up to yell, but then a noise began to come out of his mouth. It sounded all rusty and squeaky at first, but then it loosened up into a chuckle and then into a real roar that reminded me of my Uncle Elmer when he rents Pink Panther movies on Saturday nights.

We stood in amazement and watched Mr. Horvath cackle and quake. After a while he put down the note and took out a handkerchief that was red with white polka dots and wiped it across his face. Then he stuffed it back into his pocket and sniffed.

"I thought you were trying to break in or steal something," he said, his shoulders still shaking. "I didn't realize you were looking for a ghost."

Spitt jumped forward. "There's a ghost! Where is it?"

"That's not what he means, Spitt," I said.

"Has anyone died here recently?" asked Spitt eagerly.

"Not that I know of."

I knew I had better get Spitt off the topic or he might offend Mr. Horvath and ruin everything we had accomplished. As I glanced around the room I noticed the photographs again. I walked over and looked at them.

"Would you like to see those?" asked Mr. Horvath.

"Yes, please," I said.

Mr. Horvath lifted them down. Both photographs were small, black and white, and framed in silver frames. The first one was of a beautiful lady. I knew she was beautiful because I don't usually notice women at all—at least Spitt says I don't. He says I have no taste, but if I had seen her, I would have noticed. She had long black hair and dark eyes that smiled. Spitt says that eyes can't smile, but I think they can. Sometimes they smile even better than faces.

"She's pretty," I said.

"Her clothes are old-fashioned," said Spitt.

"My wife, Anna," said Mr. Horvath.

"How did you meet her?" I asked politely.

"She was the skinny little girl next door. When she came back from studying English at the university, she had turned into a beautiful woman."

"That's cool," I said.

The other photograph was of a boy about my own age. He was standing at attention, but the solemn effect was ruined because he was grinning as if he had just stuffed a live lizard down the back of his teacher's dress. He had a huge dimple in his chin and thick dark hair that didn't quite seem under control and eyes like the woman's. His clothes were plain and looked homemade, as if he had come from a farm. The pants went tight at the ankles, and he was wearing boots.

"My son, Miklos," said Mr. Horvath.

"He looks nice," I said.

"He was a good boy."

"Is he grown up now?" asked Spitt.

21

Mr. Horvath spit on the glass covering Miklos and wiped it off with his sleeve. "Oh, no," he said. "Miklos died."

"Did he die here in this house?" asked Spitt.

"In Hungary."

"I'm sorry," I said.

Mr. Horvath set the pictures back up on the shelf, side by side. "It was a long time ago."

"How long?" Spitt wanted to know.

I moved over close to Spitt and kicked him really hard on the back of the leg. This is my signal to him that he's being rude. I haven't had to do that too often—maybe once or twice in the past month.

Mr. Horvath didn't seem to notice. "He died in 1956," he said.

"Where's Hungary?" asked Spitt, aiming a kick back at my shin.

We had recently learned about Hungary in social studies. It just goes to show how well Spitt pays attention in class. "Hungary is in central Europe," I said, "and is surrounded by several other countries, including Czechoslovakia and Romania. It covers an area of approximately 92,000 square miles and, since July of 1990, is no longer ruled by a

Communist government. Its chief agricultural products are grain and sugar beets."

"Stop showing off," said Spitt.

"There was an uprising against Russia back in 1956," said Mr. Horvath, rubbing his chin thoughtfully.

"Did you drive the Russians out?" asked Spitt.

"No."

"What happened then?"

"Around that same time some friends of ours disappeared. Later we found out they had escaped from Hungary. We thought about it for a long time and decided we wanted to go too. We wanted to live in a free country, preferably an English-speaking one. We all spoke English quite well by then."

"One night we fled to Austria. Anna said to me, 'If I get killed, you take Miklos and go on. If you get killed, I go on.' It was for Miklos, you know. We wanted Miklos to grow up free."

"What went wrong?" I asked.

"We came to the border between Hungary and Austria. The border was a plowed field about twenty yards wide. We started across, crawling on our stomachs. Anna first, then

Miklos, and then me. The Russian soldiers saw us. They fired with machine guns."

"Wow," said Spitt.

"That isn't good," I said.

"Anna and Miklos were killed. I ran for it. I was in an Austrian hospital for six weeks. When I was well, I came to Canada."

"To High River?"

"To Lethbridge. I worked for two years in the sugar beet fields to pay for my passage. Then I moved to Calgary."

I couldn't keep from staring at Mr. Horvath. It was amazing what happened to people that you didn't even know about until they told you. The world was full of all kinds of strange happenings. I felt good about Mr. Horvath. I rather liked him, even though he was a bit grumpy and couldn't quit rubbing his chin. He seemed like a nice person, like my Grandfather Bates, or Stevie Fisbull's great-uncle, who gives him quarters every time he comes to visit. I could hardly wait to get home and tell Cindy she had made a mistake. It just goes to show you should never listen to rumors because usually the rumor is only partly true or not even true at all.

In either case you have been wrong about the person all along.

I glanced down at my watch and realized we were late getting to Calaway Park. "We'd better go," I said to Spitt.

Mr. Horvath followed us outside. He stood watching us, leaning against the door, looking old and alone. Spitt and I went down the steps and across the sidewalk. We reached the end of his yard and walked towards the street. By the time we got to the hedge we were thinking about Calaway Park and running like mad.

Things worked out better than I expected. Spitt got into trouble only three times and almost got kicked out of the park only once— when he climbed onto the back of the plastic swan and fell into the middle of the lake. But that was a minor mishap, forgotten in no time. And when he bought a ghost detector that was guaranteed to work under water and in subzero temperatures, I pretended not to notice. All in all, it was the best day ever.

## ≋ CHAPTER 4 ≋

"Well, it's like this," said my dad. Dad, Spitt, and I were sitting in our backyard under the cottonwood tree. It was fluffing in full force now, and the yard looked like a cotton field in the deep South. I had picked up bits of cotton here and there and already had a ball of it in my hand. Spitt was making pathways through it with his toe.

Dad said, "I can't take you boys fishing today. I have too much to do."

My dad works up north on the oil rigs and comes home every few weeks, sometimes for a week and sometimes for only a couple of days. When he comes, I always ask him to do things with me. Sometimes he does, but mostly he doesn't. He's usually too busy. It used to bother me when I was a kid, but I don't worry about it much anymore.

"Can you take us tomorrow?" I asked.

"I can't promise, Son."

My dad has hazel eyes that wrinkle around the corners when he smiles and brown hair that curls all over his head. He's always trying to straighten it with different kinds of gels and creams. He even tried a perm once because he heard that a perm would make curly hair go straight, but it just made his hair worse than ever. That was the year they used him for a sheep in the ward Christmas party.

"How about the day after?"

"I'll see how things go."

Mom always gets me to write letters and tell Dad about what I'm doing. I like writing letters, but sometimes writing letters to my dad is really hard because I don't know what to say. Sometimes I start to tell him what my friends are doing, and I realize he doesn't know who my friends are. So when I write I usually just tell him about general things like the weather and how I'm doing in school.

"See you later," said Dad.

"Yeah. See you," I said.

"What do you want to do today?" asked Spitt, after my dad had gone.

27

"Don't know."

"Have any money?"

"No."

"Me neither."

We started up the street. When all else fails, it pays to just start walking. Something is bound to turn up sooner or later. As it was, something turned up sooner than later. It turned up in the form of Mr. Horvath weeding his garden.

Mr. Horvath was hunched over the plants like a knotty old tree. His straw hat clung to his head at a lopsided angle, and he wore green gloves and a red-checked shirt with coveralls over the top. He had mud on his knees and elbows, and a big clump of it hung from the end of his mustache.

"Hi," I said.

Mr. Horvath sat back, took out his handkerchief and mopped his face with it, smearing the mud, and stuffed it back. Then he removed a package from some obscure pocket, shook out a toothpick, and stuck it between his teeth.

"Mornin'," he said.

"Do you like fishing?" said Spitt. Sometimes Spitt gets behind in conversations and keeps going, like a broken record, on things that have already been discussed. It confuses people because he quite often makes statements that are totally irrelevant to the topic at hand.

"Haven't done it for a while."

"Come with us, then!"

I could see what Spitt was up to. He was trying to get Mr. Horvath to take us fishing. It was a good idea, but it wouldn't work. Mr. Horvath was too old, for one thing. He would stub his toes on the sharp rocks and have trouble getting through the thick brush that grew along the bank of the river.

Mr. Horvath gazed helplessly around his yard at the weeds, which sprouted everywhere, and at the lawn, which resembled an enormous head of hair. "The people who lived here before sort of let things get out of hand," he said.

"Oh, don't worry about the yard," said Spitt. "Kevin and I will come by tomorrow and help you with it." Sometimes Spitt is generous, but the problem is, he's not usually generous unless it includes me. "First thing in the morning," he added.

Spitt can be pretty persuasive when he

29

wants to be. Usually half of what I do with him I didn't want to do in the first place.

Ten minutes later we were back at Mr. Horvath's with our fishing rods in our hands. We found Mr. Horvath in the backyard putting tackle into the trunk of a car. At least, it appeared to have been a car at one time. I had seen something like it at an auto wrecker's once. It was lime green and shaped like a giant Easter egg. I was willing to bet this one had been around for a long time. It was rusty, and pieces of it had fallen off. It looked to me like we'd be lucky to make it to the end of the street.

"Oh, wow!" said Spitt. "A '51 Chevy!"

I stared at Spitt.

"'51 Chevy! Isn't it gorgeous?"

We opened the doors, and they creaked. We climbed in. Dust settled as we sat. The seats were losing their stuffing. The radio had been taken apart, and bits of it lay all over the dash.

"Are you ready?" asked Mr. Horvath.

"Yes," said Spitt.

"I'm not sure," I said.

The motor roared to life. No muffler, of course. It was no less than I had expected. The brakes were probably no good, either, but at least the vehicle had a standard transmission and could be slowed by shifting down. I looked around. The gear shift was a hockey stick handle poking up through a hole in the floor-boards. I could see the gravel driveway underneath.

"It's beautiful," breathed Spitt.

"A friend of mine borrowed it for a while," explained Mr. Horvath. "He was kind of hard on it."

It turned out I was wrong about the car. I didn't think we'd make it to the river, but we did. We parked under a tree, and Mr. Horvath turned it off with a screwdriver instead of a key, because, he said, the key had been broken off inside. We left the car sitting there, clicking and popping, and headed downstream.

We walked until we found a deep hole. The only problem was, to get to it we had to walk right through the middle of a patch of yellow weeds that were swarming with bees. I hate bees. I got stung once, and ever since bees have made me want to scream and run. I would never admit that to Spitt. He takes advantage of any human weakness.

Mr. Horvath went through first, and I learned something about him. He has nerves of steel. Of course, to someone who has been shot at by machine gun bullets, bees must seem like spitballs. Spitt went through the weed patch next. I waited till he was almost across, and then I took a deep breath and ran full tilt.

"There's less chance of getting stung if you go slow," said Mr. Horvath when I reached the other side.

"Stung? I didn't think of that."

"Yes, he did," said Spitt, "but he wants people to think he's brave."

Mr. Horvath gave me one of his twitchy winks. "What is brave?" he asked. "How do you recognize true bravery?"

"That's easy," said Spitt. "It's when you do something dangerous that doesn't scare you."

"A task might frighten one person and not another."

"Some people are braver," said Spitt.

"If they both do it, then who is braver?"

"The scared one," I said.

"The one who's not afraid, of course," said Spitt.

That is another problem I have with Spitt.

He doesn't allow his brain to work properly. He just starts talking before he even bothers to think things over.

"Never mind," said Mr. Horvath, attaching a worm to his hook. "Let's get busy and catch some fish."

## ◈ CHAPTER 5 ◈

We cast our lines across the water. The day had turned out warm and windy. I was surprised Mr. Horvath hadn't lost his hat. It kept tipping but never quite blew off.

Mr. Horvath got the first bite. He brought it to shore, and it turned out to be a whitefish. A few minutes later I caught a sucker, but I threw it back. Suckers aren't good to eat, and they're so ugly it's embarrassing to admit you've even caught one. Then Spitt pulled out a rainbow trout about the size of a sardine.

"There's a better spot down this way," said Spitt.

"You go on. We'll come in a minute," replied Mr. Horvath.

Spitt took three steps in one direction and suddenly stopped as if he had come to a brick wall.

"Look what I found!" he shouted. "Look what I found!"

I glanced around, but all I saw was his rod still in his hand. "What is it? What have you found?"

Spitt turned back to us, his face like a light. "Come here and look!"

I went over. I peered down. There in the mud by the bank was a footprint made by someone who had gone swimming.

"A footprint," I said. "So what?"

"Not just a footprint!" Spitt yelped. "Can't you see that it's much too large? It's a Sasquatch print! See—look how enormous the toes are! Why, they're as long as my whole foot!"

"Forget it, Spitt," I said, flinging my line out across the water.

"I need your help, Kevin."

"No. Absolutely not."

"You're just jealous that I discovered this first!"

"I am not!"

Spitt turned and stomped away. I pulled at my line, but the hook seemed tangled in a bush on the far side of the river. That's what you get for trying to argue with Spitt and fish at the same time. I yanked it as hard as I could but it held.

"He has a very creative mind," said Mr. Horvath.

"He's been like this ever since I first met him," I said, jerking my rod back and forth.

"At least life would never be dull."

Mr. Horvath pulled in his line and looked at me while he rubbed his chin with his hand. His cheeks were all crinkled up as if he was finding something rather funny. Of course, his cheeks are quite crinkled to begin with.

"That's for sure. Last week he was investigating life on the planet Mars. The week before that he kept trying to find a man-eating spider. The week before that he went to the library and checked out all the books on the Loch Ness monster. He tried to talk his mom into flying us all over to Scotland, but she said no."

I pulled my rod high in the air and yanked with all my might. The hook released and flew back with a whoosh, barely missing my head. Now that I thought about it, I remembered being told that this sort of thing was dangerous because you could end up with a hook planted in the side of your face.

"Oops," I said.

"I think you're too hard on Spitt," said Mr. Horvath, chuckling. "After all, he's just a boy with a good imagination. Tell me, how did he get the nickname 'Spitt'?"

"That's because of me," I admitted. "His real name is Montgomery, after his great-grand-father, but he never liked that name, and he doesn't like Monty, either, because he thinks it sounds too girlish. Then last year he became so good at shooting spitballs that he could hit a target better than anyone else in the fifth grade. When I started calling him Spitt, just for fun, everyone else started doing it, too. The only person who didn't like it was his mom."

"I can understand that," said Mr. Horvath.

I stuck on a new worm and tossed my line back into the water. "I still think it sounds bet-ter than Montgomery," I said stubbornly.

"Now that I've learned something about Spitt, tell me about yourself. What do you like to do? What is your family like?"

"Well," I began, reeling in my line for another try, "I like mathematical things. I want to invent something when I grow up. I like studying about rockets, too."

"Good for you," said Mr. Horvath. "And your family?"

"I have a sister and a mom and dad. My sister is a pain, and my mom and dad are much too strict. They never let me have any fun."

"Of course not," said Mr. Horvath. "Isn't that the way moms and dads always are?"

"Mine especially, because we belong to the Mormon church. We have all kinds of rules, you know."

"I've heard of the Mormon church," said Mr. Horvath in a polite way. "You go to church in a temple."

"Oh, no," I quickly explained. "We go to church in a regular church. In the temple, people get married for eternity, and the children they have belong to those parents forever."

"I see," said Mr. Horvath, but I could tell that he really didn't see at all. His forehead was wrinkled up, and he was gazing out over the water with his eyes all squinty as if he had suddenly thought of something he didn't like. I decided now was a good time to change the topic. I pulled in my line.

"This isn't a very good fishing spot," I said. "Let's go find Spitt."

Mr. Horvath and I eventually met up with Spitt by the golf course. I had fished in this particular place before. Mom and Cindy had even come with me one time and splashed around and scared the fish away. Things looked good today, though. No one in sight.

Spitt grinned when he saw me. One thing I like about Spitt—he never stays mad for long. I think he forgets to be mad. I don't think his mind wants to be bothered with concentrating on one thing for that long at a time.

I watched as Spitt leaned forward and threw his line as far as he could. It was a pretty good cast, and I heard it plunk far out across the water. He began reeling it in, and suddenly he started to whoop and yell and pull at the line, which had gone taut in his hands. I scrambled up the bank.

"Careful, now," I said.

"Don't lose it," said Mr. Horvath, coming up from behind.

"Not too fast," I said.

"Don't let the line go slack," said Mr. Horvath loudly.

"A little to the left," I said.

"Bring it in faster," said Mr. Horvath even more loudly.

Mr. Horvath leaned out over the water with a net. The trout swam closer. We saw its gills heave, and its stripe shimmer in the sunlight. A rainbow trout!

That's when everything went wrong. The first thing that happened was the trout slid under the water and disappeared. The next second the surface of the water opened up and out came a shark. It wasn't a real shark. It only looked like one. It was an enormous pike with a mouthful of wicked teeth, and between those teeth was clamped Spitt's trout, like a mouse in a trap.

"Oh, no!" I yelled.

"Let me get him with the net!" shouted Mr. Horvath.

"He's eating my fish!" screamed Spitt.

That's when the bank gave away. We didn't think about not jumping and screaming all together on the very same spot. It was an honest mistake, Mr. Horvath said afterwards, one that anyone could have made. After that, we caught a lot more fish. The fish bite much better when you're right down there with them.

## ≈ CHAPTER 6 ≈

"Aaa . . . aaa . . . choo!"

Mom removed the thermometer from under my arm and held it up to the light. "Just as I thought," she said. "One hundred and one."

"Then I can't go outside?"

"Not until this fever goes down."

She had that certain tone in her voice. I've come up against that tone before, and there's no way of fighting it. It's the tone she uses when she's not going to change her mind.

I lay down and pulled the blankets up to my chin. My window faces the street, but it's way up high and I have to lean out to get a view. All I could see from my bed was a piece of blue sky and a cloud that looked like a castle.

I sure hoped Mr. Horvath hadn't caught a cold. I wasn't worried about Spitt. He's as healthy as a bulldog and never catches anything that comes around. He didn't even get the mumps last winter when I had them. He came up to my room and stood at the foot of my bed and told me how much fun he was going to have cross-country skiing without me. The only consolation I had was he fell over a ledge into some deep drifts and had to be pulled out by his Uncle Heber, whom he dislikes immensely. His pride was the only thing that got hurt.

I glanced around my room. I had it arranged just the way I liked it. A Canadian flag hung on one wall, and a poster. The poster was a blown-up photograph of the first oil rig my father ever worked on. It was an old diesel-powered one, and there aren't many of those left around. My baseball glove and ball lay on the floor along with a whole pile of dirty clothes. Books and cards rested in various places. Mom says I should be more careful with my things. She says she could take half my stuff to the dump and I wouldn't even notice, but that's not true. I have a place for every single thing.

In the summer I share my room with a family of spiders. They come in through a hole in the corner. I usually let them be unless they start crawling all over me. Every now and then an ant or a beetle puts in an appearance on its way to somewhere else. I draw the line at mosquitoes and bees.

I relaxed and gazed through the window. The castle had turned into a kettle-drum. Everything was quiet. I could no longer hear Mom clanging pots downstairs or Cindy's radio blaring in the background. Cindy always picks the most terrible stations to listen to. She has no taste. Just like that spider over there who is eating a fly. Who would want to eat a fly . . .

The next thing I knew I was awake. The reason I was awake was that someone had tapped against my bedroom window. I crawled out of my bed and lifted the window. Spitt scraped down the shingles, grabbed the ledge with his hands, rolled in, and fell with a thud and a grunt onto the floor. That is not a new thing for Spitt. He quite often comes in by climbing up the tree and running across the roof. He prefers it to using the front door. He says it's quicker because he doesn't get held up by Mom or Cindy or whoever else is around at the time.

"Good morning, Spitt," I said.

"It's afternoon," he said, standing up and brushing off his clothes. "It's just like you to be hiding in here while I'm out working myself to death."

"Working?" He did look a bit frazzled. His face was red and sweaty, and his jeans were caked with dirt and pieces of grass. He had a mosquito bite on the tip of his nose.

"Yes, working. At Mr. Horvath's, like we promised yesterday. Where have you been?"

"Mom won't let me out of the house. I have a fever."

"You look fine to me."

"I feel fine, but I'm starved. Want to come downstairs?"

"Sure."

I found my tennis shoes hidden in a corner under my Gretsky sweat shirt. I put them on, and together Spitt and I thumped down the stairs and into the kitchen. No one was there.

"Oh, darn," said Spitt. "I was hoping your mom had baked cookies."

I rummaged through the fridge and found an apple and a hunk of cheese. I left my mom a note. It said, "I'm fine. I went for a walk with Spitt. I'll be back soon. Love, Kevin."

The air outside was thin and hazy. Up in the afternoon sky hung an orange sun, bright as a

Chinese lantern. A faint tinge of smoke stung my nostrils.

"Forest fires," said Spitt.

"It's been too dry," I said.

"That's for sure."

"I hope it rains soon."

"Me too."

Alberta sometimes gets forest fires in the summer if it doesn't rain for a long time. I always worry about it because I think, What if the firemen can't stop the fire, and it comes and burns down High River? But they must know what they're doing because it hasn't happened yet.

"Come over here. Mr. Horvath wants to see you," said Spitt.

He opened Mr. Horvath's back gate. Mr. Horvath beckoned to us from his chair in the shade. There was a pitcher of lemonade and some glasses laid out on top of a cardboard box. I gazed around. The lawn was mowed; weeds lay in heaps all over the garden. I was impressed.

"Kevin," said Mr. Horvath after we had discussed the yard, the weather, and my health, "last night I went to the library and read about the Mormon church. I would like to learn more. There are some things that puzzle me."

I stared at Mr. Horvath in disbelief. No one had ever asked me anything like this before. Dimly, as if from a distance, I heard Spitt hiss into my ear. "Close your mouth, Kevin! You look dumb!"

I coughed and covered my mouth with my hand. I took a deep breath. "Do you mind if I get my mom to phone you?" I managed to sputter. "I don't know very much, but when it comes to religion, my mom knows everything."

"Everything?"

I looked at him and saw the twinkle in his eye. I laughed out loud.

"EVERYTHING," I insisted.

"Well, then," he said, "I must certainly talk to her!"

The following week dragged by so slowly that I hardly lived through it. Mr. Horvath dropped in a few times, had big long conversations with my mom, and took away armfuls of Church books, only to bring them back later and trade them for new ones. Spitt came over every day but kept disappearing without telling me where he was going. I made a few trips to the river on my bike with my rod but never got even a bite. Finally I became really desperate and spent some time cleaning my room.

It was on the extremely boring Saturday morning at the end of this same extremely boring week that Mr. Horvath found me trying to raise the seat on my bike. I had yanked too hard on it, and my fingers were all practically broken.

"It's stuck!" I yelled, standing up and giving it a kick.

Mr. Horvath put down his books and gripped the seat between his hands, carefully attempting to move it this way and that. He seemed to be thinking more about other things than about the bike. He said, "Kevin, your mom told me that when you were eight, you got baptized."

"Yes," I said. "My father did it." I looked to see if Mr. Horvath was making any headway, but it was too hard to tell.

"Your mother says after that you were different."

Definitely, the seat was moving higher.

"Kevin?"

"Uh, yes. I remember. I received the gift of the Holy Ghost. After that I would get feelings about whether things were right or wrong. My mom says that's how the Holy Ghost works, and I should always do what it says."

"Do you?"

"Well, I . . . "

At that moment Spitt came clamoring up the driveway on his bike, waving his arms and shouting while his bike wobbled like a top in a slow spin.

"Kevin! Come with me! I have something to show you!"

Mr. Horvath handed me my bike, which was fixed just the way I had wanted. "Here you are," he said.

"Thank you, Mr. Horvath," I said. "I really appreciate it. I hope you enjoy those books." I waved back at him as I rode away.

Spitt's destination proved to be none other than his own backyard. "Look at this," Spitt said to me.

I looked at it. "It" was a rectangular wooden frame built out of studs and covered with plywood.

"What is it?" I asked.

Spitt's eyes glowed like live wires on a dark night. "A Sasquatch trap," he said.

"How does the Sasquatch get in?" I asked.

Spitt reached down and pulled back a piece of board. "He'll go in there. Then I'll close it up."

"Do you think the plywood will hold a Sasquatch?" I asked, walking around the contraption and trying to appear as if I was taking it all seriously, which I wasn't.

"Mr. Horvath said it would work as well as anything else."

"That makes sense," I said.

"Mr. Horvath said he would take it down to the river for me when he gets the chance," Spitt explained. "In the meantime, I want to do a test run so I'm better prepared for the real thing. Can you come over Monday night and help me keep watch?"

"That's family home evening night."

"Tuesday, then?"

"Well, uh . . . uh . . . "

I tried to think of something that might be happening on Tuesday night. My brain clicked wildly and came up blank.

"Thanks, Kevin," said Spitt in his most grateful tone of voice. "You won't regret it—I promise!"

## ❖ CHAPTER 7 ❖

On Sunday Mr. Horvath went with us to church. Spitt's parents came too, which doesn't happen very often, and we filled up the whole bench. Mr. Horvath was dressed in a black suit that had thin places in the elbows and knees and a very wide checkered tie. Spitt tried to get him to trade ties, but Mr. Horvath declined.

The chapel was so hot I could hardly breathe. There has always been a problem with the heating system in our building. In the wintertime, the air conditioning comes on. During the summer, the heat kicks on. This was June, and there was definitely a lot of heat coming from somewhere.

Mr. Horvath sat beside Spitt and me. Sometimes, when I'm not very interested in what is going on, I whisper to Spitt and he whispers back. Today, however, I wanted to be a good example to Mr. Horvath. I didn't talk, not even when Spitt poked me in the ribs and Cindy stepped on my foot going past. There was a good feeling in the meeting, especially when one of the speakers talked about the Prophet Joseph Smith. On the way home, I walked with Mr. Horvath. I was afraid to ask him if he liked it. Then after we had eaten dinner and after the grown-ups had finished visiting and Mr. Horvath had finally gone out the door, Mom called us all over and said, "Mr. Horvath has asked to take the discussions."

She didn't even get mad when I leapt over the sofa and did three cartwheels across the living room floor.

On Tuesday I asked her about going with Spitt.

"Fine," she said, leaning over her dresser top and applying a dab of green shadow to her left eyelid. "But wear your gray sweater, in case it gets cool, and be back in early. It's not wise for boys and girls to be out alone after dark."

"Boys—and girls?"

"I don't want you leaving Cindy alone while we're at this discussion with Mr. Horvath. She's too young."

"Cindy will ruin all my fun," I said, trying to sound firm.

"I could hire Mrs. Tofsrud."

Mrs. Tofsrud is six feet tall and has hands like the paddles of my dad's canoe. "I'll take good care of Cindy," I said.

I took three steps toward the door and suddenly realized that Spitt and I hadn't been invited to the discussion. I stopped dead in my tracks.

"How come Spitt and I aren't invited?" I demanded, hoping I sounded justifiably insulted. "We're his best friends, you know. If it hadn't been for us, you wouldn't even know him!"

"The missionaries thought it wasn't a good idea," said Mom, dabbing at her nose. "They wanted this to be a spiritual experience."

Dusk had arrived. Spitt and Cindy and I were crouched under a bush in Spitt's backyard, and I was extremely uncomfortable. My right leg had gone to sleep, and my left one had a cramp. Cindy was ramming her elbow into my rib cage, and Spitt was breathing into my left ear. I hate hot air going into my ear. It tickles like mad.

"Move over," I said to Cindy.

"I can't. There's no room."

"This test run is a waste of time," I said. "Everyone knows Sasquatches don't come into towns, and even if they did, they'd never play baseball."

Spitt had used his own baseball bat for bait. Spitt's baseball bat is not an ordinary bat. It is an aluminum bat with yellow fluorescent lightning bolts painted on each side. His dad gave it to him when he turned twelve. Spitt worships it. It can knock a ball farther than any bat in town. Spitt calls it The Bomb.

"Sasquatches are just more careful when they come into towns," said Spitt. "And The Bomb will work—trust me. The Sasquatch will think it's the best hunting club he's ever seen."

"What if it's a girl Sasquatch?" asked Cindy.

The moon was out. It slid across the evening sky like a giant ball of red fire. Smoke hovered in the air in hazy layers of yellow and gray. There was no wind. I could feel the darkness around me like a hot heavy blanket.

"How long have we been here?" I asked.

"Five minutes," said Cindy.

"It's very dark," I said.

"You have to be patient," said Spitt. "These things take time."

We waited. Sparrows chirped in the stillness. A cat meowed. The lights in Spitt's house blinked on.

"Maybe we should go inside and wait," I said, leaning from one cramped foot to another. They were like pincushions would be if they could feel.

We waited. Next door, a car pulled into Mr. Horvath's driveway. Two men climbed out. It was easy to tell they were Mormon missionaries. They had on white shirts and ties and carried scriptures in their hands. I could see my father and mother walking up the sidewalk to meet them.

"They're going in the house," said Spitt.

"Who is the red-haired one?" I asked.

"It's Elder Anderson, the new elder who talked in church last Sunday," said Cindy. "Boy, do you have a lousy memory."

"Oh," I said. "He looks different somehow."

"Shh!" said Spitt. "There's something coming!"

We waited. At first I couldn't hear or see anything out of the ordinary and thought he might be seeing things, which isn't uncommon for Spitt. Then out from behind the far side of the house a dark shadow parted itself from all the other dark shadows and began to drift across the yard, a huge hulk floating through the thick night air.

I shivered in the heat. "I think I'll go now," I said.

Spitt grabbed my arm. The colossus moved closer. Cindy's fingernails dug into my right shoulder blade. Spitt's hot breath seared the back of my neck. I forced myself to watch. There are a lot of things I know and a lot of things I don't know, but one thing I know for certain is that all kinds of bad things can happen in the dark. There was something scary and dangerous out there, and I wasn't too keen on finding out what it was.

The blob grew clearer. It arrived at the trap. Its thick arms hovered. There was something about the way it moved, something vaguely familiar. If only I could figure out what it was. The plywood tore away from the frame with a screech. The Bomb rose into the air. The shadow turned, and I saw its face. It wasn't a Sasquatch. It was worse than a Sasquatch. It was Marvin Ritchie.

Marvin Ritchie is the meanest kid in town. He's bigger than everyone else and gets into lots of fights, and he always comes to our end of town and walks past our street on his way to the arcade. Sometimes he takes things that don't belong to him, and most of the time he gets away with it because kids are afraid of him. He's built rather like a football standing on end, and he has muscles that bulge. He has pale little eyes with no eyelashes and a head that is harder than granite. One time Stevie Fisbull hit him on the skull with a tennis racket by mistake and he hardly even noticed. It hurt the racket worse than it hurt Marvin.

"It's Marvin Ritchie," I said.

"He's taking The Bomb!" yelled Spitt.

"Let him," I said.

Spitt sprinted across the backyard. I followed at a safe distance. Cindy covered her eyes and stayed where she was. She was being smart for a change. This was serious business.

I felt quite confident about how things would turn out. Spitt has never been famous for being a hero, and he never picks a fight unless it's with someone he can outrun. That's why I was sure he would pull back at the last minute and let Marvin Ritchie go. No one in his right mind ever picks a fight with Marvin.

Spitt launched himself at Marvin. That's when I remembered that you can't judge Spitt by the same rules you judge other people by, but it was too late. Marvin Ritchie had seen the danger and was advancing. Just as Spitt flew forward with his arms groping, Marvin's massive bulk turned in a circle, gathering momentum. Marvin's great elbow cleaned Spitt out of midair as a sharp razor wipes stubble from a chin. Spitt hit the ground and curled like a salted slug. I was coming close behind. Marvin Ritchie's hands still held The Bomb, moving in a circle, forming a perfect swing. I was running too fast to stop. My face was heading right for The Bomb, which was just completing a three-hundred-and-sixty-degree arc. The last thing I remembered thinking was it was too bad my head wasn't a baseball. It would have been a home run.

## ≈ CHAPTER 8 ≈

The only thing good about it was I got lots of attention. The first person to visit me the next morning was my dad. He was on his way somewhere, and I guess he figured he owed it to me to stop in. The doctor had kept me in the hospital one night to make sure I didn't have a concussion, he said. My dad came tramping in, looking impatient and out of place, and sat on the edge of a chair.

"Well, Son," he said. He always calls me Son when he's being formal. The rest of the time he calls me Kevie. I hate the name Kevie because it makes me feel like I'm two years old. I would rather have him call me Son than Kevie.

"Hi, Dad," I said.

"You've been chasing Sasquatches, I hear."

Sometimes my dad teases me. I don't like it

because it makes me feel dumb. I usually try to pretend it doesn't bother me.

We sat for a while, neither one of us talking. Dad cleared his throat and put one leg over the other. The problem with me and my dad is we don't know each other very well. I used to cry every time he left, but that was when I was a little kid. I'm too big to cry now.

"Are you going somewhere today?" I asked.

"I'm slipping up to Edmonton for a few days."

My dad travels a lot. I guess the oil companies need their people to go a lot of different places. My dad is an engineer, but I've never been able to figure out exactly what he does. He never talks about it to me.

Dad stood. He had to look a long way down to see me, he was so tall. He was holding his jacket, and he kept moving it from arm to arm. He said, "Try to stay out of trouble, Son." Then he turned away. I couldn't tell if he was joking or if he was serious. He didn't look at me when he said good-bye.

I lay in the hospital bed for a while and didn't think about anything at all. The bed beside me was empty. Sunlight poured through the window, thick with smoke. The sky was heavy and gray.

I watched part of the twelve o'clock news. The fire damage to Alberta's forests was getting alarmingly high. It was too depressing to think about, so I changed the channel. All that was on was a soap opera. I was already feeling plenty nauseated so I turned it off.

Mr. Horvath came next. I was surprised to see him. I guess I just wasn't expecting him, that's all. He sat down in a chair and leaned back with his feet resting on the edge of my bed as if he figured the least they could have done was provide him with a footstool.

"How are you?" he said.

"Fine," I said.

Mr. Horvath cleared his throat and frowned at me from under his eyebrows. He wasn't really frowning, I could tell. His face was frowning, but the rest of him wasn't. I've learned with Mr. Horvath that means he's got something on his mind that he's getting ready to let out.

"I met your father outside," said Mr. Horvath.

"That's nice," I said, staring at a spot on the ceiling.

"He asked me to watch out for you."

That is something I can't understand about my father. If he thinks I need watching out for, why doesn't he stay and watch out for me instead of doing all those other things that are more important?

"I'll be all right," I said, staring at a place on the wall behind Mr. Horvath's head.

"Oh, I'm sure you'll be all right," said Mr. Horvath. "I'm not so sure about your father."

"He'll be fine," I said. "He really enjoys his work. He never does anything else."

"That doesn't mean he enjoys it."

"Of course it does! Adults always do what they want!"

Mr. Horvath laughed, but it was an empty, vacant sound, like something tapping on a tin roof. "At your age, it must seem that way," he said.

"I've got a headache," I said, staring at a spot on the floor. "This conversation is giving me a headache."

"I'm surprised a headache is all you have," said Mr. Horvath, "with a lump of that size."

We sat for a while not speaking. I looked at Mr. Horvath from out of the corner of my eye. He was rubbing his chin with his hand, and his sparse white hair was combed down against his scalp, making his head seem too small for the rest of him. His hands were thin, and you could see the blue veins like little rivers under the skin. His knuckles were like big knots of rope.

He stirred and said, "I almost forgot. I brought you something." He took a book out of his pocket. I reached for it. I have always loved books, even when I was a small child and used to write in them. I always got in trouble when I wrote in them. Mom could never understand that I wrote in them because I loved them.

The book was called *Successful Fishing in Tributaries of the Bow River,* by Art Heninger. There was a pike the size of a shark on the front cover. Two men were holding it up.

"Thank you," I said, hardly daring to touch it.

"You're welcome," said Mr. Horvath in a gruff voice.

I looked through the pages. Some passages were underlined in red, and some places were marked where Mr. Horvath must have figured I would need to pay closer attention.

"I thought you'd like it," he said.

"Thank you," I said again, placing it reverently on the nightstand by my bed.

We talked for a while longer about fishing and about baseball. I must have fallen asleep sometime during the conversation because the next thing I knew I woke up and Mr. Horvath had been replaced by two people who were standing beside my bed, gawking down. If I hadn't been so sleepy, I probably would have jumped a foot into the air. As it was I just lay like a lump and stared.

"Hello, Kevin," said Marvin Ritchie.

It was Marvin Ritchie and his father. Marvin Ritchie's father is a bigger, rounder version of Marvin. He has ears that poke straight out from the side of his bald glossy head and a red nose that looks like a cherry—without the stem, of course. Although sometimes, if I try really hard, I can almost picture the stem. His lips are thick and wet like Marvin's.

"Marvin has something to say," said Marvin's father.

Marvin's lower lip hung low. "I'm sorry I hit you in the face with the baseball bat," he said. "It was an accident."

"I know," I said.

"Marvin wants to make amends for his disgraceful behavior," said Marvin's father. "He wants everyone to know that he is going to make some changes in his life."

Marvin stared at the floor and kicked at the bedpost with the toe of his shoe. "I'm having a birthday party next week," he muttered. "You and your sister are invited." The last part of his sentence sounded as if he had almost choked getting it out.

"Thanks," I said.

Mr. Ritchie reached over and patted my arm with his damp puffy hand. "We'll see you then," he said.

"Yes. See you then," I said.

After they had gone I lay and stared at the ceiling. A party at Marvin Ritchie's! It has always been my lifelong dream to see the inside of Marvin Ritchie's house. I've ridden past it hundreds of times. It's on the east side of town, and it has a round tower going up one side. People say Marvin's grandmother died in the tower. No one I know has ever been inside the house. Everyone at school talks about it because it is the house the movie men used for

Lana Lang's when they filmed *Superman III*. I remember when they made that movie because they painted a huge American flag on the side of the furniture store, and it took a whole year before they finally got around to painting it over. Half the kids in town got to be in the movie as part of the crowd, and they even got paid. I tried out but didn't make it. That's usually how my luck runs. Cindy got to be in the movie, and she didn't let me forget it for the next three months.

"How are you feeling, Kevin?"

"Hi, Mom," I said.

Mom reached down and placed her hand on my forehead. Mom always puts her hand on my head when she's worried about my health. It's a compulsion she can't seem to get over.

"How are you?"

"Fine."

"I'm not very happy about this."

"I know."

Utter humility works the best with Mom. I stared at my hands, which were folded on my lap, and hoped my lower lip was trembling just enough to make her feel sorry for me. I have to be careful with this sort of thing. If I lay it on too thick and heavy she gets suspicious. Now was definitely not the time to bring up the subject of Marvin's party.

"We've been invited to a party!" bellowed a voice. The door of my hospital room flew open, swinging wildly. Something thudded against a wall. Something scraped across the floor. It was Spitt. He crashed in, threw his sweater and shoes on the bed, plopped himself onto a chair, and draped one leg up over the side. "I can't believe it!" he exclaimed. "A party at Marvin Ritchie's!"

Mom looked from Spitt to me and back again. "A party? When?"

"This Saturday."

"I don't believe Kevin will be well enough to go," said Mom.

The thing I had to remember was not to panic. If I panicked, then all was lost.

"I'll go by myself, then," said Spitt.

Something snapped inside of me, like a rubber band suddenly letting go. I grabbed the nearest thing I could find, which turned out to be my pillow, and threw it with all my strength at Spitt. "You traitor!" I screamed. "How dare you! It's your fault I have two black eyes! I didn't want to catch a Sasquatch—I don't even believe in Sasquatches! Then I was being a good friend and trying to save you from Marvin Ritchie, and what do you do? You say you're going to a party—MARVIN RITCHIE'S PARTY—without me!" I stopped, but only because I had run out of air and there were little silver stars dancing in front of my eyes.

Mom pushed me back down onto the bed and put the covers over me. "It's all right, Kevin," she said. "I'll think about the party."

Mom and Spitt looked at each other as if they were in on some great secret that was beyond my capacity to understand. Spitt stuck out his lower lip and wrinkled his forehead the way he does when he's trying to look superior. "Sometimes Kevin gets upset about things," he said.

Mom smiled. "Only when he's not feeling well."

Spitt crawled across my bed, reaching for his sweater and shoes. I tried to kick him from under the blankets, but they were too heavy and I couldn't get my foot to gather any momentum. All I managed to do was make a lump.

"I'll come by tomorrow," said Spitt, heading for the door. He had almost reached it when he turned and looked back at Mom. His jaw was set and his brow furrowed, like a wise monk contemplating some deep truth. "You know, Mrs. Thompson," he said, "this is why Kevin needs me so much. I'm such a good friend to him during the hard times of his life."

## ❂ CHAPTER 9 ❂

"They're fighting the fires with fire now," I said.

Spitt and I were walking past Mr. Horvath's house. The air felt dry and scorched, like trying to breathe in a desert. I didn't want to do anything vigorous for fear it would hurt my head. I had to be very careful with my head; it wasn't quite back to normal. Spitt said I looked like a raccoon, but then he exaggerates a lot.

"How do they do that?" asked Spitt.

"They start a fire in front of the other one so when it gets there there's nothing left for it to burn."

"Does it work?"

"Of course it does. Why else would they do it?"

Mr. Horvath's place looked deserted. Spitt and I walked into the yard. The ground was speckled with a few apples that had fallen from the tree.

Spitt picked one up and stuck it in his mouth. I crammed three into my pocket for later.

"I wonder where Mr. Horvath is," I said.

"Probably visiting someone," said Spitt.

"He doesn't usually do that."

"Maybe he went to get the mail."

"Maybe," I said.

I went to Mr. Horvath's door and knocked. I peeked through a window. I walked around to the garage and stepped inside. The car was still there. I looked under it and in the backseat. You can never be too careful these days. I saw a movie once about some thieves who tied and gagged a fellow and hid him in his own car.

"I guess he's not here," I said.

"Let's come back another day," said Spitt. "Maybe he'll be back by then."

That's when Mr. Horvath's scrawny head poked up suddenly from behind the front fender of his car.

"Hello, boys!" he exclaimed. "You're just in time to help me polish my car!"

I tried to decide which would be best, to feign sickness or to flee, but before I could do either, Spitt grabbed my arm and pulled me back. Moments later Mr. Horvath provided us with rags that looked like what he was wearing, just a little more tattered, and a bucket of yellow goop he called car wax. We dipped in our rags and set to work.

"Should I polish the rust spots?" I asked. This was a completely reasonable question, I figured, since my part of the car seemed rather severely afflicted.

"Rust?" Mr. Horvath mumbled. "What rust?"

I polished as best I could around the big brown spots that weren't rust. After a while my arm began to ache. I switched to the other one. As I moved toward the front of the car I noticed a Book of Mormon lying on the dash. Mr. Horvath must have seen me looking at it because he said, "I read it while I drive."

I stared in horror at him until I realized that the strange gurgling sound I heard was actually Mr. Horvath chuckling, and his face wasn't turning purple from a breathing difficulty but from sheer mirth.

"Very funny, Mr. Horvath," I said in disgust.

"What's so funny?" asked Spitt from the far side of the car.

"Mr. Horvath is reading the Book of Mormon," I explained, "and he tried to tell me . . . "

"Do you like it, Mr. Horvath?" interrupted Spitt. "I tried to read it once, but it was too hard for me."

Mr. Horvath's face suddenly grew serious. "It reminds me of the Bible. When I read, it feels like God is speaking. But I get frustrated with the people who are called Nephites. When they are righteous they are blessed with gold and silver and great wealth, but they never stay righteous for long."

"Gold and silver?" said Spitt, his head popping up between the front and back doors. "Where is their gold and silver now?"

"Dead and buried, like they are," I said gruffly.

"Lost, I would imagine," said Mr. Horvath.

"Lost things can be found," said Spitt eagerly. "Do you think any of the Nephites lived around here?"

"Of course they didn't live here!" I hooted.

"I've been thinking a lot about the Nephites, myself," said Mr. Horvath. "They were interesting people."

We spent the next hour talking about the Book of Mormon with Mr. Horvath. I never did figure out what to do with the big brown spots.

The night of Marvin Ritchie's party finally arrived. Mom had decided I was well enough to go after all. My eyes had turned all kinds of colors, but the swelling had gone down. I still had a headache, but I didn't tell Mom. She has a tendency to become agitated over such trivial things.

Half the neighborhood was going to Marvin Ritchie's party. Mr. Ritchie had hinted that Marvin was tired of being disliked and wanted to make some new friends. Spitt figured he was having the party so he could get lots of presents. I disagreed with him. Sometimes I think Spitt dwells too much on the negative side of human nature.

Cindy was excited about going. I could tell she was excited because she wouldn't quit talking. When Cindy gets excited, she talks, and she had been going steadily since breakfast. Personally, I can't figure out why anyone would want to have a birthday party and invite sisters. The only thing that made any sense to me was that Marvin's parents were in charge.

74

Some grown-ups don't understand about this sort of thing.

Spitt and Cindy and I went together. Mom couldn't drive us because she had to leave early to meet my dad. He was returning from his trip to Edmonton, and Mom had to go to Calgary to the airport and bring him home. Spitt's father and mother were working and couldn't get away, so we were on our own. Mom made us promise to stay together.

"Of course we will," I said.

We dressed up in our good clothes and tucked the presents under our arms. We left the house and headed east past the hospital and toward the railroad tracks. Thick black clouds loomed above the mountains behind us. The streets and buildings were dreary and gray, as if someone had taken a garden hose and washed out all the color. It was damp and sticky and warm. Everything was still, as if waiting.

"This is creepy," I said.

"Maybe it will rain," said Spitt.

"The weatherman said there was a 95 percent chance of rain," said Cindy. Cindy always watches the weather. I can't think of anything more boring than watching the weather.

"I hope it puts out all the fires," said Spitt.

"The weatherman hoped so, too."

We walked a few more blocks. It's a long way to Marvin Ritchie's. We walked through downtown and over the railroad tracks and past the police station. A police car pulled up to the station, and an officer got out of his car. The gun he was wearing made me think of Mr. Horvath and how scary it would be to have someone shoot at you.

"I'm going to join the Royal Canadian Mounted Police when I grow up," said Spitt.

"I'm going to be a model," said Cindy. "What are you going to be, Kevin?"

"I don't know."

"Kevin's going to be a scientist," said Spitt. "He's going to save the world from nuclear destruction."

"Is that true, Kevin?"

"Spitt is exaggerating," I said. "I would like to be a physicist."

"What's a physicist?"

"Someone who does scientific things like saving the world," said Spitt.

We could see Marvin Ritchie's house in the distance. The tower rose into the sky like a lone lighthouse on an empty sea. The moon was just coming up, and it lay on the far horizon, red and swollen. Clouds rolled in the sky. Trees moved like shadows in Marvin Ritchie's yard. I thought about Mr. Horvath when he escaped from Hungary, running alone through a dark empty night. I shivered and walked a little faster.

## ≈ CHAPTER 10 ≈

We moved quickly up the front walkway. Branches reached like arms. Twigs plucked like eager fingers. The porch creaked under our feet. Light from the windows spilled across the lawn in a pale eerie haze.

Spitt rang the doorbell. We waited. He rang it again. The door squealed open. Surrounded by a harsh explosion of light, color, and sound stood Marvin Ritchie himself.

He had a piece of chocolate cake in one hand and a strawberry sundae in the other. The front of his shirt was soiled where he had spilled something green on it, and when he spoke the words came out muffled by food.

"Did you bring any presents?" he spluttered.

"Of course we did," said Spitt, bounding past him and into the room. Cindy and I followed close behind. I closed the door behind us and then stood, leaning against it, feeling strange and uneasy. Something was wrong. I had no idea what, but something felt wrong somewhere. A lump had started to form in the pit of my stomach, a sick heavy lump that was threatening to ruin my appetite. I took a look at all the marvelous food and decided what I wanted to do with this illness was ignore it.

Marvin grabbed our gifts and disappeared into the crowd. An enormous lady smiled and handed us plates. We heaped them high. A movie banged and bellowed in the next room. Party games roared around us. Music blared in the background.

"Wow!" said Spitt. "This is a dream come true!"

I took a heaping bite of cake with frosting and ice cream. It stuck in my throat and wouldn't go down because my stomach, which should have been waiting quietly to receive it, was rolling around like a log in white water. I set my plate of food down and swallowed. The food lurched up and down three times before it finally settled.

When I was eight years old my father baptized me and gave me the gift of the Holy

Ghost. Ever since that time, things that are good make me feel really good, and things that are not good make me feel uneasy. Sometimes I even feel sick. Right now was a definite sick.

"Spitt," I said, "we have to go."

Spitt looked at me and then whooped with laughter. "That's a good joke, Kevin!" he said.

"We have to go, Spitt," I insisted. "Something is wrong, and I think it might have to do with Mr. Horvath because I can't quit thinking about him. We have to go see if he's all right."

"How do you know something is wrong?"

"I just have a feeling."

Spitt stared at me until he saw that I was really serious. Then he turned all red in the face and started waving his arm around—luckily the one that wasn't holding his plate of food.

"Are you crazy!" he yelled. "This is the biggest party of the year! There are hot dogs and ice cream and cake with chocolate frosting! Clark Kent himself stood in this house! Think of what we'll miss!"

"I'm not leaving," said Cindy. "You can't make me!"

I stood and looked pleadingly at Spitt and Cindy. They set their jaws and looked sternly back at me. I sighed, turned, and went to the door. I swung it open. It closed behind me with a final-sounding thunk.

I walked alone as the sky grew darker. The moon struggled to peek through a mass of thickening clouds and then gave up altogether. Lightning flickered and snapped, and high up in the sky I could hear the beginning of thunder, like the first growl of an angry lion, like the rumble before the volcano erupts. I broke into a run.

My sister caught up with me just as it started to rain. I looked over my shoulder in amazement at Cindy and shouted, "Why did you come? You'll miss all the fun!"

"Because Mom said I should stay with you!" Cindy shouted back. "And because, well, when you left alone, I knew you weren't kidding!"

"How?"

"Because everyone knows you're afraid of the dark!" she hollered above the wind.

"I am not!" I yelled. "Whoever told you that?"

The rain came slowly at first, in little splatters and gusts, and then increased, as if someone had just begun to tip a bucket. We ran faster.

"This is the stupidest thing I have ever done!" Cindy gasped a while later.

"I disagree," I wheezed. "I can think of many things you've done that were more stupid than this!"

Cindy glared. Then, in spite of the rain and the cold, in spite of everything, we burst out laughing.

Ten minutes later we weren't laughing anymore.

"My side hurts," croaked Cindy. She was gasping like a fish on a bank, and her hair hung down on her shoulders in little soggy strings. I was gritting my teeth and squinting my eyes to keep the water from running in. We reached the end of our own street.

"Let's hurry!" I whooped.

"I can't go any farther!" wailed Cindy.

"Sure you can!" I cried.

Cindy came to a dead halt and sank weakly down onto the sidewalk. I grabbed her and pulled her up by the arm. She tried to push me away. I started to yell at her to get up, and she started to scream at me to leave her alone, but it was all lost in the sound of the sky falling apart. At the same time the crash of thunder hit, a flash of deathly white lit up the world like an exploding bomb, and then it was over. The thunder stopped, the lightning ceased, and the rain let loose as if a dam had broken. And every light in High River went out.

## ◈ CHAPTER 11 ◈

"It's locked," I said.

I had managed to drag my sister to the opposite side of the street, and we were huddled in front of our own house. We decided that since the power was out, the next thing to do was find a flashlight. I had two in the bottom drawer of my dresser, and when I admitted that to Cindy, she said she had known for a long time that I was hoarding flashlights. I told her that I wasn't hoarding them at all. I simply had them there in case I wanted to read under the covers late at night. Then she asked me when was the last time I did that, and I said it was last week, if she had to know. She told me to prove it. That's when I decided the conversation was going nowhere.

I tried the front door, and it was locked. We weren't at the party where we were supposed to be, and Mom thought we wouldn't be where we were, so what did I expect?

"Of course it's locked," Cindy said. "Mom always locks it when she leaves."

"What are we going to do?" I wondered.

I went over to one of the basement windows. I had seen my dad take out a window once when we were spring cleaning. I found a stick floating in a puddle that was fast turning into a lake and fiddled with it at the window like my dad had done. It had taken my dad about five seconds to get the window out. All I received for my efforts were two squished fingers and a bruised knuckle.

"It isn't working," said Cindy.

"I've almost got it," I said.

"How about if I try?" said Cindy, squinting down at the window.

"If I can't do it, then you certainly can't," I said. "It's a known fact that boys have better motor skills than girls."

"We'll see," said Cindy. "Don't stand in my way like that. I need more room."

Cindy took the stick with both hands and did basically the same thing I had done. I whistled and looked around. I leaned from one foot to the other. This was a total waste of time, but I had to humor her or she'd pester me for hours.

I heard something thunk to the ground. "I'll be back in a minute!" she said. She was on her hands and knees with one foot already inside. I stared in amazement.

"There are two flashlights in my bottom dresser drawer," I said when I could finally speak. "I want the big one! It's waterproof and has batteries that can be recharged!"

I stood and waited. I stayed close to the wall where the roof hung over and the rain couldn't get on me. Not that it mattered. I was already pretty well soaked. In a minute I saw a light moving past the windows inside the house, and soon afterward Cindy came out the front door. She had both flashlights, and she gave the big one to me. "Now," she said, "at last we're ready."

I led the way. We dashed across the street without looking for cars, because there were none—nobody else was stupid enough to be out. We ran through a yard, down an alley, around a hedge, and finally clambered over the picket fence that separates Spitt's yard from Mr. Horvath's. We started through Mr. Horvath's garden and sank to our knees in puddles of water and mud that seemed like quicksand.

"I lost my shoe!" cried Cindy, tugging at my sleeve.

I swung my flashlight back around. We looked up and down every inch of the black mucky row as the water beat on our backs and in our eyes and dripped off the ends of our noses.

"Got it," I said. "Let's get out of here."

We plunged out of the garden and across the grass, sliding more than running. We stumbled up to Mr. Horvath's back door and stopped. His shoes lay on the ground, side by side and filled with water, like two small sunken boats. A shovel was propped up against the house, and from the top of it hung his straw hat, the one he always wears, dripping like a rag on a scarecrow. The catch on the door hadn't held. A gust of wind caught it, threw it open, and then slammed it back in our faces. I grabbed it in mid slam and almost lost my balance. I banged on the door, wondering if he would even hear. I banged again. I shouted his name, and then Cindy and I shouted together.

"Come on," I said.

We stepped inside and closed the door behind us, tight this time, so it would stay in place. We tiptoed across the porch and into the kitchen. We huddled together and pointed our flashlights. The window was open, and the curtains billowed in and out, like a ghostly robe. Raindrops splattered in on the floor.

"Someone is here," whispered Cindy. "Someone is watching."

"Marvin Ritchie," I said. "I'll just bet it's Marvin Ritchie."

"Impossible," said Cindy. "He'd never leave all that good food."

"You might have something there," I said.

We stood in silence and listened. The house seemed to groan and creak. Dark shadows fled across ceilings, chased by our feeble lights. A tree branch scratched against the window like fingernails down a chalkboard.

The hair rose on the back of my neck. My teeth chattered, and every muscle in my body started to wiggle and jump. It felt like the time I slept on one of those beds you find in motel rooms. You can put in a quarter and for a few minutes the bed shakes you to pieces. That's what I was doing now. I was shaking to pieces.

"Someone is watching us," repeated Cindy.

I opened my mouth to yell at my sister. I wanted to tell her firmly to stop all this stupid nonsense, that there was no one here and no one watching us and if she was trying to scare me it certainly wouldn't work and she might as well quit when I looked over to the other side of the room, the part of the room by the doorway leading to the stairs going up to the next floor. Something dark hovered for a moment and then soared up the stairway and was gone. It must be a robber, I decided. There was no other explanation. My heart felt as if it would pound through my chest, but the feeling was even stronger that I had to find Mr. Horvath.

"This way!" I exclaimed, sprinting for the stairs. Cindy stared at me with wild eyes, but she followed me. Partway up I began to wonder what the chances were of the robber sneaking around, coming up from behind, grabbing me around the neck, and choking me senseless. I shone my light back behind me just to make sure.

We reached the top and started down the hallway. The robber was nowhere in sight. I had slowed my pace to a crawl and took each step with deliberate care. Cindy's face shone pale as the moon as she gazed over her shoulder and frontward again.

"Are you afraid, Kevin?" she whispered.

"Only a little bit," I chattered.

We were almost halfway down the hall. Five doors led off to rooms, and I checked each one with great care. The first room on the right was an empty bedroom. The first door on the left was a bathroom. The second door on the left was another bedroom, completely empty except for a rolled-up rug in one corner. The fourth door, the second on the right, must have been the bedroom Mr. Horvath used. It had an old bed and a dresser with a broken mirror and a closet with a few lonely clothes drooping from limp hangers.

"We'd better not stare," I said to Cindy. "It's not polite to look at other people's things."

I barely got out the words. In fact, I might have still been pronouncing the last few syllables. Cindy was looking at me and I was looking at Cindy so neither one of us glanced up until it was too late. When we did, the robber was right there in front of us, all black and covered with mud and slime and shouting loud horrible words.

He came toward us, waving and jumping. Cindy screamed. I froze, unable to move. "Run for it!" I yelled. "Run!"

It was like my worst nightmare, the one where I'm trying to run from some terrible monster but can't get myself to move, the one where the faster I run, the slower I go. I willed my left leg to take a step. It jerked forward. I commanded my right leg to lift itself off the ground. It twitched and slid along the floor. I struggled on, and then I felt the robber pulling at my shirt. I plunged forward with all the strength my muscles possessed and broke free. I took two mighty leaps and was just starting on a third when the robber got me with a tackle from behind.

## ≋ CHAPTER 12 ≋

The robber had his elbow in my ear. The robber had his knee jabbed into the middle of my spine, and I couldn't breathe for the pain. His soggy clothes were dripping cold water and mud down the back of my neck. I tried to get up, but his heavy shoulder rolled against me, smashing my face into the floor.

"Ouch!" I said.

"Are you all right, Kevin?" asked the robber. "I'm sorry to come running out like that, but there's something scary in that room."

I slithered out from under the rolling, squirming body of the robber and grabbed my flashlight. I shone it right in the robber's face. The robber was my best friend, Spitt Wilburson himself, the one who had not stayed at Marvin Ritchie's party, after all.

"Spitt!" I howled. "What are you doing here? You scared us! We thought you were a robber!"

"I was following you," he answered reasonably, as if he followed people through raging thunder, black nights, and torrential downpours every day of his life. "It was more fun than staying at Marvin Ritchie's party ALL BY MYSELF!"

"Spitt," I said, ignoring his remark. "What did you say about that room you just came out of?"

"I heard something in there," said Spitt, shivering in spite of himself. "Something that sounded like a monster breathing."

I almost knocked Spitt over in my rush to get past him. I didn't even give myself time to be afraid. I threw myself into the room, halted, and swung my flashlight from corner to corner. On one side, almost against a wall, lay Mr. Horvath's body in a crumpled heap. It was very still.

Spitt and Cindy were close beside me as I knelt over him. I shone the light into his pale face. I touched his stone-cold hand.

"Is he dead?" whispered Spitt.

"Put your head on his chest," said Cindy.

93

"I'll check his pulse," I said, fumbling around for the proper spot on his wrist.

At that moment Mr. Horvath's eyes flickered open.

Cindy screamed, Spitt yelled, and I jumped two feet into the air. He stared up at us, blinked and moaned, and then his eyes fell shut again. That's when I knew he was in real trouble. The Mr. Horvath I knew would have barked at us, chewed us out for shining the light in his face, and ordered us to help him up. A quiet moan was not like Mr. Horvath. Not at all.

"Spitt," I said, trying to keep the panic out of my voice, "go downstairs and phone the ambulance."

Spitt's eyes were two dark craters in his moon-pale face. "Do you know the number?" he croaked.

"I do!" cried Cindy. "We learned it in school. I'll go with you!"

I listened until their footsteps died away to the floor below. I took off my jacket, which was still sort of dry on the inside, and covered Mr. Horvath. I took his hands and gripped them tight. At least he would know he wasn't alone. I stayed that way until my legs started to tingle. I changed position and felt the blood rush through them like hot needles.

The light from my flashlight seemed to be growing dim. I looked around the room. Shadows loomed and grew; strange shapes crawled out of corners. I moved a little closer to Mr. Horvath and felt him stir. I looked into his face.

"Kevin," he whispered.

"Yes," I quickly said. "It's me. Everything is under control, Mr. Horvath. We're taking you to the hospital. Don't be frightened—I'm sure it's nothing serious. We just want to make sure you're all right."

"Kevin," he said, "I was cleaning the walls . . . fell off my stool . . . felt something snap when I hit the floor. Couldn't make it to the phone." His voice was shaky and kept fading in and out. I had to lean right over him to hear.

"You're going to be fine," I said, wishing I believed what I was saying.

Mr. Horvath's voice scratched on. This was good. At least while he was talking he wouldn't die. People can't die while they're talking, can they?

"Been here a long time . . . prayed that some-one would find me. Must have fallen asleep . . . dreamed. Anna stood in the room here beside me. She was still young and beautiful . . . she was sad because I was in pain. She said she loved me."

He paused for a moment, breathing hard. "I dreamed about Miklos next. He stood near . . . saw him clearly. Told me he was happy . . . said he missed me . . . His face was like a light." A pause, another deep breath. "Before he left, he seemed restless and his eyes grew anxious. Said the strangest thing . . . said, 'Papa, you need a ceiling.' Kept saying it over and over . . . seemed so worried. 'Papa, you need a ceiling.' Then he was gone. Been thinking about it for hours . . . What did he mean, a ceiling? What does a ceiling have to do with anything?"

We sat for a few moments in silence because my throat had such a big lump in it that I couldn't speak. Finally I managed to rattle a few words out past the lump. "Mr. Horvath," I croaked, "I learned about this in Primary, and I don't think he was talking about a ceiling in a house. I think he was talking about a temple sealing."

Mr. Horvath took a few more haggard breaths. I listened anxiously to make sure the breaths didn't suddenly cease altogether. He said, "What is a 'temple sealing'?"

"Remember when I told you about parents getting married in the temple for eternity and children being with them forever?"

"Yes," he whispered.

"They call that a temple sealing."

My flashlight was practically finished. We sat there in the gloom listening to the moaning wind and the dying rain and the creak of old walls and floors around us. He said, his voice thin and hoarse like the wind outside, "It's all true, then . . . the Godhead . . . the Prophet Joseph Smith . . . the Book of Mormon . . . temples. It's all true, isn't it?"

"Yes, Mr. Horvath," I whispered, suddenly filled with a deep joy that made my eyes go all watery and made me think of my mom, who always cries in church because she's happy. "Yes," I said. "It's all true."

As we sat together on the cold hard floor waiting for the help Spitt would bring, it suddenly came to me that the dark was not nearly as frightening as it had seemed.

## ❖ CHAPTER 13 ❖

It wasn't long before I heard a siren wailing up the street. The siren cut out abruptly in front of Mr. Horvath's house. The front door banged open. Feet rushed up the stairway. Two men with a stretcher burst into the room, followed by Cindy and Spitt.

The men pushed me aside and knelt by Mr. Horvath. They immediately began to wrap long things around him and poke all sorts of sharp things into him.

"Don't do that!" I bellowed at them. "He's already in enough pain!"

They ignored me. After talking to someone on a radio, they put a mask over Mr. Horvath's face. He struggled weakly for a moment and then relaxed.

"Now look what you've done!" I shouted, jumping up and down. "You've killed him!"

"Someone get that kid out of here," said one of the men through his teeth.

Spitt took my arm and pulled. "Come on, Kevin," he said. "You've got to leave this to the professionals."

"How can we be sure they know what they're doing!" I ranted.

Spitt led me out into the hallway, where we waited. I paced back and forth frantically while Spitt and Cindy stood wide-eyed and silent. Pretty soon the men went past us carrying Mr. Horvath on the stretcher. We followed them out to the street. They put him into the ambulance. Then they climbed in and drove away.

The Trans-Alta Utility Company must have been working overtime because at that moment all the lights in High River came back on. Spitt and Cindy and I stood and squinted at each other in the glare. The street light above us seemed as bright as the afternoon sun.

"It's nice to be able to see again," I said.

"I think the storm is over," said Spitt.

We stood quietly for a moment, lost in our own thoughts.

"I'm sure Mr. Horvath will get better," I said, trying to swallow the lump in my throat.

"Of course he will," said Spitt. "He's tough."

"Are you going back to the party?" I asked Spitt.

"I think I'd rather go home."

"Me, too," said Cindy. "I'm cold."

"I'll walk with you," offered Spitt. "Are you coming, Kevin?"

"In a minute," I said.

After they left, I went back into the house. Some of the lights had come on. I stood in the kitchen for a few moments, gazing around. I went over to the shelves that were built into Mr. Horvath's kitchen wall. I reached up and took down the picture of Miklos, the one Mr. Horvath had shown to me and Spitt. I studied the dark eyes, the enormous grin, the dimple that almost split his chin. I felt that if I looked long and hard enough, he would step out of the picture, still laughing, and bid me a good evening.

"Miklos," I said. "My name is Kevin. I'm looking forward to meeting you some day."

I put the picture back on the shelf and made my way up the stairs. I stood alone in the bedroom, feeling sad. Pieces of a broken stool lay in one corner. I wondered if Mr. Horvath had been afraid, lying alone in this room all that time. It made me think of how quickly he could have been gone, without my even having the chance to say good-bye. It made me think of how quickly anyone could be gone. It made me think of my own dad. I shivered and left the room, turning out the light as I went.

I made my way back down the stairs and out through the kitchen. I closed Mr. Horvath's outside door, making sure it wouldn't blow open behind me. When I turned for home, I looked up and saw someone running down the sidewalk toward me.

It was a man. The man was tall and had curly hair that dripped and stuck to his head and shoes that sloshed when he stepped. His big chest heaved as if he had just run a race, and his jacket hung open in the front, showing a sodden shirt that was stuck to his skin. The man was my father.

I have developed a system over the years for rating the level of my father's anxiety under stressful conditions such as this. One to three is mild and not to be taken too seriously. Four to seven has to be handled with caution. Eight to ten is the high danger zone, with ten being the area of optimum danger. This was definitely a peak ten. I decided the best way to handle this difficult situation was to adopt a low-key manner.

"Hi, Dad," I said.

"Where have you been!" bellowed my dad. "Not at the Ritchies', where you were supposed to be! Not at home, although you left a trail of mud from one end of the house to the other! And where is your sister, anyway? You were given responsibility for her safety!"

My dad was advancing. I didn't think now was the time to tell him the mud was Cindy's fault. I took a step back and almost tripped over a porch step.

"What were you doing? Your mother is worried sick, and I've been searching the streets for you! Tell me right now, young man, and MAKE IT GOOD!"

I have learned that when all else fails, when you're backed into a corner and it looks like the end is in sight and it seems there is nothing you can possibly do to save yourself, when it looks like the whole mountain is about to tumble down on top of you, it always pays to tell the truth. So I told the truth.

"Mr. Horvath got hurt," I said, "so we left the party and came here to help him, and I think he's going to be all right, and you don't need to worry about Cindy because Spitt already took her home."

I smiled bravely and continued. "And, well . . . I've just been thinking about Mr. Horvath and how terrible it would be if something like this happened to you, or even something worse than this, and I never got to see you again, so I just wanted to tell you that I . . . that I . . . I . . . l-love you." My voice trailed off into an embarrassed silence.

My dad looked at me long and hard. He looked at my face, and he looked into my eyes. He took another step forward. He was right in front of me. I closed my eyes, fearing I was finished. I waited. I cringed. Nothing happened. I opened one eye just a crack.

He couldn't have looked more surprised if I had kicked him in the stomach with a boot. He stood and watched me, looking worried and relieved all at once, and then he finally said, "I love you too, Kevin."

I opened my eyes all the way. The crisis was over. My dad was no longer mad. The danger was past. I started to go around him but he reached out and grabbed me. For a second I thought my life was finished after all, until I realized he was doing something he hadn't done for a very long time. He was giving me a hug. Lucky for me he had calmed himself down. As it was I barely survived. The hug nearly broke all my ribs.

# ≋ CHAPTER 14 ≋

The last Saturday in November, we all gathered at the meetinghouse for Mr. Horvath's baptism. Mr. Horvath had given the missionaries no end of trouble. At first he had wanted to be baptized in the river, right at the place where he and Spitt and I had fallen in, but the doctor wouldn't let him get baptized until his cast came off. By that time it was so late in the fall that the missionaries were afraid the cold water would cause him to have heart failure as soon as he was submerged. After a lot of mumbling and complaining, he consented to be baptized in the font.

My father walked with Mr. Horvath down into the water. They stood together all in white while my dad spoke the prayer. I was worried for a moment that my father was holding him under too long and he would surely run out of air and expire, but he came up again still breathing and looking very happy.

Afterwards we ate doughnuts and talked about the fun things we would do during the Christmas holidays. Then Spitt pulled me aside.

"Kevin," he said, his eyebrows puckered seriously, "I've been thinking a lot about this. You know that hill behind Marvin Ritchie's house, the one with all the lumps and rocks and gopher holes in it?"

"Yes," I said, reaching for my third chocolate doughnut with sprinkles on top.

"Well, I've been thinking, and I'm sure there are Nephite warriors buried under that hill. I'm sure lots of gold and silver is buried there with them, and I would like to go there and dig next spring when the ground starts to thaw."

"Spitt," I said in my most assertive-sounding voice, "I've also done a lot of thinking about this, and I've decided . . . "

At that instant I looked across the room and caught Mr. Horvath's eye. It hit me that if he had known what I was about to say to Spitt, he would have been disappointed in me. The words died in my throat—all the words that said searching for Nephite gold and silver is the stupidest thing I have ever heard of and I won't do it and go away and leave me alone until you come up with something more sensible. I remembered how much Mr. Horvath liked Spitt and that he always said Spitt was just a boy with a good imagination.

I looked back to Spitt, cleared my throat, and made a quick revision to my previous statement. "Spitt," I said, "I've noticed that a lot of valuable things in historical times were buried in hills. Why, even the gold plates were buried in a hill. This is an extremely valid theory you have come up with."

I stuffed the last bite of my third doughnut into my mouth and seriously considered a fourth. Spitt stared at me for a long moment in disbelief that gradually changed into unabashed joy.

"Will you come with me, then?"

"Of course I will," I said. "But only if you get Mr. Ritchie's permission. It's not right to trespass."

Spitt beamed. "I've already talked to him. In exchange, all he wants us to do is help landscape his yard!"

Mr. Horvath will never know the magnitude of the sacrifice I have made.

# ◈ ABOUT THE AUTHOR ◈

Vicki Blum is a school librarian and has published many stories in the *Friend* magazine. She graduated from Ricks College and from Athabasca University and now lives in High River, Alberta, Canada, with her four children. In her spare time, she enjoys boating, horseback riding, and hanging out in used-book stores. A member of The Church of Jesus Christ of Latter-day Saints, she has served as a ward Primary president and as a Sunday School teacher of fourteen-year-olds. The *Trouble with Spitt* is her first novel.